SANTA S.O.S.

by Linda Ford

AN
APPLE
PAPERBACK

SCHOLASTIC INC.
New York Toronto London Auckland Sydney
Mexico City New Delhi Hong Kong

To my sister, Marti Ann Ford
Thanks for everything

No part of this publication may be reproduced in whole or in part, or stored in a retrieval system, or transmitted in any form, or by any means, electronic, mechanical, photocopying, recording, or otherwise, without written permission of the publisher. For information regarding permission, write to Scholastic Inc., Attention: Permissions Department, 555 Broadway, New York, NY 10012.

ISBN 0-439-12911-7

12 11   4/0

Printed in the U.S.A.   40

First Scholastic printing, November 1999

CONTENTS

CHAPTER 1

Santa Disappears

I'll never forget the day Santa Claus disappeared.

It was early in December, and I was at my parents' flower shop, getting ready to make some deliveries. My twin sister, Marcia, was there, too.

I'd been delivering flowers for a couple of years now. In September Marcia had asked if she could do it also.

"Absolutely not!" Dad had pounded the kitchen counter to make his point.

"But Nick's been doing it for two years."

"Nick's a . . . I mean . . . that's different."

"You mean, Nick's a *boy*."

"Well . . ." Mom had joined the conversation. "It *is* different for boys and girls, dear."

"That's medieval!" Marcia proclaimed.

"That's the way it's going to be in this family!" Dad declared. Which didn't make any sense, considering everything, but it made him feel better to lay down the law. He and Mom stayed firm, too, so Marcia was stuck.

They let her work in the store, though, and she'd developed a tidy side business on her own. She decorated the shop Christmas tree with red velvet bows (she called them "maroon"), lace, and other dried flower junk. A brainstorm had hit her in October to offer "decorator" Christmas trees.

Incredible as it seems, she'd already gotten twelve orders, and this kept her dashing to the craft shop for more ribbon.

"Talk about old-fashioned," I told her while she was making lace angels.

"So what?"

"How are you going to convince Mom and Dad you're all modern and independent while you're doing stuff from the nineteenth century?"

"I don't have to prove anything."

She was probably right about that. But I still thought it was funny.

"You'll be laughing out of the other side of your mouth when I get through." She smirked.

"I'm going to make at least as much on Christmas trees as you do on tips."

"No way!"

"Wanna bet?" she asked.

"Ten bucks says I make more. But it has to be *real* profit. You've got to take out everything you spend on lace and ribbons and junk."

"Well, you have to take out everything you spend keeping that bicycle going."

"Done."

We shook hands on it. After I'd thought about it for a while, I was sorry. Marcia's good at everything that has to do with Christmas. Good thing, too, since that's her career choice. But in the meantime, I'd have to pedal my legs off to beat her.

Anyway, that's why we were both at the store when the call came in about Santa Claus.

Dad put down the receiver, and I noticed his eyes were kind of glassy. And he was totally silent. That was a first. Dad *always* had plenty of words for every occasion, even the time I accidentally knocked down the emergency brake and the car rolled into Samsonville Pond.

Finally, he mumbled, "Santa is missing."

Mom's chin started to wobble. Then she clenched her teeth and swallowed hard. Mom gets misty-eyed over sentimental stuff, but she's pretty tough when there's a crisis.

I gulped and suddenly felt sick to my stomach.

"Ha-ha!" a raucous voice made me jump. It was Stanley "Stinko" Jones. The sneer on his face made my skin crawl.

"What's the problem, Mr. Martin?" he drawled. "Did your Santa Claus crash his sleigh?"

"None of your business, Stin . . . Stanley." I corrected myself at the last minute. Dad didn't like it when I used Stanley's nickname.

"Well, I might be able to help you," Stinko said, putting his elbows on the counter and looking face-to-face at Dad. Even though he was in shock, Dad automatically moved back. Stinko hadn't gotten his name for nothing — his breath could stop a truck. "The way I see it," he continued, "if you need someone to play Santa here at Fantastic Flowers, just rent me a costume. I know that routine."

Believe it or not, Stinko could probably pull it off. We were in the same class at school, although he was a year and a half older. They *said* he'd been sick as a baby and didn't go to school till late. Even so, most twelve-year-olds couldn't do Santa.

Stanley could.

He was really big, and he was really lazy, which

was the only thing that kept him from being the school bully. So he just flapped his mouth and was a general pain in the neck. His dad was the school janitor and played Santa at the mall every year. After kindergarten, I refused to have my picture taken with Stinko's dad. Bad breath runs in that family.

Stinko hung around the shop a lot. He knew I made good money on tips, and he wanted in on the action. I don't know why he bothered. If there were deliveries I couldn't handle, I always called in my best friends, Jake and Matthew. But he hung around anyway, and we ignored him most of the time. It was like he wasn't even there. Which is why Dad had slipped during his conversation on the phone. Usually he's very security conscious.

"We'll call you if we need you," Mom managed to tell Stinko. "I think you'd better go on home."

With an elaborate shrug, he oozed out of the door.

"What do you mean, he's disappeared?" Mom demanded.

"I don't know. That was the message."

Now, it was a good thing that Stinko thought we were talking about a hired Santa Claus. If he'd realized we were speaking about the real thing, he probably would have called the police and had us locked up in the loony bin. After all, who still believes in Santa Claus when they're as old as Mom and Dad? For that matter, who believes in him when you're ten, like Marcia and me?

Stinko doesn't know the facts. And he's not *ever* supposed to know the facts. After all, Santa Claus is the *real* family business.

CHAPTER 2

More Bad News

You see, Santa Claus is my grandfather.

Like I said, it's a family business. When Granddad wants to retire, my father will take over. I should have been the next in line since I'm the only boy in the family — my parents didn't have the good sense to have more than one son. Instead they had Marcia and me, and then *three* more girls. They're happy, so I won't complain anymore. Well, not as much as I used to.

Anyway, I was supposed to be Santa in the future. Except I want to be an oceanographer. Not that the family agreed with my career choice. I even went through apprenticeship Santa training last summer. It was a disaster. I get airsick. I'm allergic to reindeer, and besides we hate one another, especially Donner and I. I don't get along with the North Pole staff, either. Like the time I tried to computerize the office and they all went on strike. *They* got the best of it. Granddad hates computers as much as they do. Added to that, I'm lousy flying the sleigh, and I'm scared of heights. My *only* qualification is that I'm a night person. Dad and Granddad aren't. They hit the sack early.

Forget the milk and cookies routine for Santa Claus. Granddad needs coffee. *Strong* coffee.

It turns out that Marcia's good at everything I'm not. So, after some arguing, everyone agreed that Marcia could be Santa after my father. She's an incredible sleigh pilot, even better than Granddad.

But now Granddad had disappeared.

This is *not* like my grandfather. He's predictable. He's always on time. Actually, he's always early. Something was really wrong if Grandma didn't know where he was.

"Could the sleigh have broken down?" Mom asked.

"Maybe that's it," I agreed.

I was lying. Through my teeth.

Believe me, that sleigh can't break down. It's the most amazing piece of technology I've ever seen. My great-great-great-great-grandfather invented the antigravitational system back in the 1840s, and we haven't had a malfunction yet. Except I could hardly say that to Mom; it would scare her even more.

"That's probably what happened," Marcia agreed with a firm nod. "You know, the sleigh can't possibly crash, but there's a lot of small things that could ground it for a little while. And remember that Granddad's no good with a screwdriver. He'll have to wait until a maintenance crew can get to him. I sure don't envy them. He'll probably be foaming at the mouth."

I was impressed.

Marcia's voice was so cool, I expected to see icicles dripping from her lips.

Mom and Dad believed her, but underneath, I could tell that Marcia was plenty worried.

The bell tinkled as the door was opened by a customer.

"May . . . may I help you?" Mom asked. She sounded almost normal. Quietly, Dad told me to finish my deliveries and get home by half past five. Grandma was going to call and give us the details.

"Dad," Marcia said, "I'm going to go with Nick."

"Sure, sure," he mumbled, and turned to deal with a second customer.

Marcia helped me load the flowers into the cart attached to my bike and then followed on her own.

"What do you think?" she asked as soon as we were out of earshot.

"Can't tell until we know more. But it doesn't sound good."

"It *can't* be the sleigh," she asserted.

"You don't need to tell me. I kept wishing the thing would break down last summer, and it never did. It's built too well."

We finished the deliveries in record speed. At 5:25 we raced into the driveway and up to the office where we kept the North Pole phone.

There wasn't anything wrong with the sleigh. Granddad had taken the team out for a little exercise. The reindeer had eaten too much for Thanksgiving dinner, and he'd figured they needed to get in shape for Christmas Eve. They'd headed in the direction of Chicago.

The team came back to the North Pole. Granddad didn't.

And the Police Think It's a Joke

"I'm going to the North Pole," Dad announced.

"Me, too," I added.

"Count me in," Marcia said.

Mom looked like she wanted to say the same.

"Don't be silly," Grandma said over the speakerphone. Marcia and I made a face at each other. We'd be left at home twiddling our thumbs, without a thing to do. But Grandma surprised us. "There's nothing you can do here, Nicholas," she continued — my dad's name is Nicholas like me, but she usually calls me Nick, or sometimes Nicky. "Marcia and Nicky should come."

"But, Mother," Dad started protesting.

"But nothing," she told him firmly. "You've got

responsibilities at home with the flower shop and the other children."

She had him there. Fantastic Flowers couldn't close down at this season, and Mom couldn't handle it alone.

"I'll tell you what you can do, Nicholas," Grandma said. "You take Nicky and Marcia to the plane in Chicago, then you can check around for any information that might help."

"Well, okay, Mom," Dad replied, obviously relieved that there was *something* he could do. I knew how he felt.

Mom phoned the airline for plane tickets to Norway, where our charter service would pick us up. She managed to get us on a flight leaving midafternoon the next day. Marcia and I packed while Dad went to fill the car with gas. If we started right away, we would get to Chicago by midnight. We'd check into a motel and then stop by the police station in the morning.

"Yes?" The woman at the counter of the police station seemed to be in a hurry.

"My father is missing," Dad told her.

"For how long?" She sounded like she took a thousand missing person reports every day. Maybe she did.

"A day and a half now. . . . He was . . . uh . . . traveling in the Chicago area when he . . . uh . . . disappeared."

She raised her eyebrows. "Perhaps he just extended his trip."

"Oh, no!" Dad exclaimed. "He's missing; he'd never just leave his . . . uh . . . vehicle. . . . I mean he . . ."

"You found the abandoned car? What's the license number?"

"It isn't a . . . uh . . ."

"I'm sorry, ma'am," I stepped forward and said. "My father drove all night, and he's pretty tired. The thing is, my grandfather always checks in on time. He'd never let my grandmother worry like this, so we know something must have happened. Isn't there anything you can do?"

"All right. His name?"

"Nicholas Martin."

"Age?"

"Fifty-seven," Dad managed to say. He probably felt as foolish as I did. We couldn't exactly tell the woman that Granddad flew a sleigh and that the reindeer came home without him.

"Here. Fill out this form and turn it in, with a picture if you've got it."

There were a lot of questions, some about us

and some about him. Dad bit his lip when he came to the part about what clothing his father was wearing when he disappeared.

"So," the woman said when she read through the form. "He was wearing a red winter suit with black boots. Does he also have a long white beard?"

She seemed to think it was a joke. She was *not* amused.

"No beard . . . although he might have been wearing a fake one. . . ." Dad's voice trailed off at her icy stare.

"Look, mister. I'm sick of this joke. Every year someone thinks it's oh so funny to make a missing person Santa Claus report. You're a little early, though. We usually hear from you jokers closer to Christmas."

"It's not a joke, really, it's just that . . ."

"Believe me, mister, it isn't a joke. Filing a false police report is serious business. You're wasting police time, and you could be charged with a crime."

"It's not a false report," Dad gasped.

"Come on, Dad," Marcia said, and grabbed the form. She told the woman, "We'll get back to you later."

In a way, I could hardly blame the police-woman. We couldn't tell her the truth, and the parts we could tell sounded awfully fishy.

We spent the rest of the morning calling hospitals. One said they had an unidentified man who matched our description, so we rushed over there. But it wasn't Granddad.

"You know," Marcia said on the way to the airport, "I'm almost sorry we're the ones going to the North Pole. You'll probably get a call saying Granddad's back, and we won't know about it because we'll be on the airplane."

She didn't sound very convincing. Still, I kept hoping she was right and there'd be a message waiting for us in Norway.

There wasn't.

CHAPTER 4

What I Didn't Know at the Time

"Ouuuuchhh!" Granddad felt the lump on his head. "What happened?"

"Hello," said a voice.

He scrambled out of the snowbank and saw a little girl about seven or eight. "Hello," he answered. "What's your name?"

"I'm Jessica," she told him. "And I already know who *you* are."

"You do?" Granddad scratched his aching head. The girl knew who he was. That was good, because *he* didn't know! He couldn't remember his name or who he was or where he came from. "Who am I?" he asked her.

"You're Santa Claus," she replied. Then she

leaned forward and whispered, "Don't worry, I won't tell anyone you're here."

Granddad smiled. She was a cute little girl, with brown pigtails and dark brown eyes. He looked down at himself. No wonder she was confused. He *was* wearing a red suit and black boots.

"I'd better go," Jessica said. "I'll see you on Christmas Eve."

Granddad sighed. He'd have to go into town and ask around. One of the stores had probably hired him to play Santa Claus. They'd know who he was.

He walked into the town and saw a sign that said HUNTSVILLE. The name didn't sound familiar. After a while he came to a large department store.

"Am I your Santa Claus?" he asked one of the salesmen.

"Huh?" the salesman said. He was very busy and barely stopped. "Our Santa is over there." He pointed to a big cardboard sled where people were taking pictures of their children.

Granddad walked all over town and asked at every store he found. Everyone already had their Santa Clauses or they hadn't hired one yet. But he *was* offered two jobs for the Christmas season.

"I have an idea!" he said to himself. "I'll go to

the costume shop. I must have rented this costume from *someone*."

The bell of the costume shop tinkled like a Christmas chime. An old man sat behind the counter.

"Did I rent this costume from you?" asked Granddad.

"Don't you remember?" the man asked back.

"To tell you the truth, I don't," he answered. "I had a little accident, and I can't remember my name. But I thought I might have rented this costume from you, and you'd know who I am."

"Wish I could help," said the man. "But that's not one of my costumes. It's much nicer than anything I've got for rent."

Granddad was disappointed. "Are there any more costume shops in town?"

"Nope. I have the only one."

"Thanks anyway," Granddad said as he headed outside. It was getting dark, and he didn't know what to do. Besides, his head was hurting. Up and down the streets he walked, looking at faces, thinking maybe he would recognize someone. He didn't.

It grew very late, and all the stores closed. Granddad headed for the park, figuring he'd have to sleep on a bench. He was lucky the Santa Claus suit was so warm, but he'd rather have a bed.

In the middle of the night someone shook his shoulder. "Wake up, old man," a voice said. "You can't sleep on park benches." It was a policeman.

Granddad groaned. Where could he go?

He walked around some more and found the bus depot. He was so tired he just sat right down on a bench, leaned against a wall, and closed his eyes.

The next morning, he felt stiff and sore from sleeping while sitting up. He groaned and straightened himself.

"Hi, Santa," a cheery voice called.

He blinked his eyes and looked across the room at the woman behind the ticket counter.

"Hello," he managed to say.

"Are you okay?"

"Well . . . I had some kind of accident yesterday, and I can't seem to remember my name."

"What did the police say?"

Of course! He felt foolish. His family must have told the police he was missing. All he had to do was go to the station. He probably could have spent last night home in bed instead of sleeping on a bench!

"I'm going over there right now."

"Good luck."

He had to stop to ask for directions, but it was

only a short way. He walked inside, butterflies twitching in his stomach.

"Am I missing?" he asked the woman at the desk.

"You don't seem to be," she answered.

"No . . . I mean, has someone reported me as missing? I hit my head yesterday, and I can't remember my name."

"How about Santa Claus?"

"Very funny."

"Sorry. Were you wearing that costume when you got hurt?"

"Yes."

"Okay. I'll check the missing person reports. Have a seat in the waiting area. I'll find someone to take your fingerprints."

Granddad sat in the waiting area. There were some wanted posters on the wall. It gave him a creepy feeling. How did he know if he was wanted or not? Maybe he was a terrible criminal. Maybe that was why he was wearing a costume — to hide who he was!

He tugged at his fake beard. He didn't want to turn out to be a bad person.

Not being a criminal was definitely better than *being* a criminal.

Especially when you're sitting in a police station.

CHAPTER 5

Things Haven't Changed Between Donner and Me

Seeing the sleigh brought it all back to me.
The nausea, I mean.

I didn't even have to ride in it. Just *seeing* it was enough to make me airsick. And a bit wobbly in the knees.

I'm not a coward. Really. At least I don't think so. I ride in planes with no problem; my bedroom's on the third story; and I can do more stunts on my skateboard than any guy in my school. Plus, I'm the only one in my house who'll empty the mousetraps. I just don't like going up in a sleigh flown by reindeer. There's nothing to hold you in.

Hmmmm. A thought nibbled at the edge of

my brain, then slid away when I saw the reindeer wranglers eyeing me.

By now, Granddad had probably gotten around to telling the North Pole staff that Marcia was going to be Santa instead of me — and I'll bet they all cheered when they heard the news. We didn't exactly get along last summer. But hopefully Granddad hadn't told them I was nervous about heights. That'd be too embarrassing.

To preserve my pride, I pretended to be casual, stomping around the sleigh, pretending to do a preflight inspection. Everything was always in place, but it never hurt to check. I stopped beside Donner.

"You imbecile," I growled. "How could you possibly come home without Santa Claus?"

Donner made a whiny, woofing sound and hung his head below his knees. He was the perfect picture of a devastated reindeer with a depression complex. I didn't buy the act for a minute, but the wranglers did.

"Cruelty to animals," one of them muttered to another.

They all gave me a dirty look.

Terrific. Donner screws up and comes out smelling like a rose. And everybody still hates me.

The wranglers shook their heads sadly and

marched toward the air control tower. As soon as their backs were turned, Donner's hind foot went flying, and so did I.

"Something wrong?" Marcia asked. She'd come around the front of the sleigh.

I spit out a mouthful of snow. "Nothing," I said with dignity.

She raised her eyebrows, but I wasn't about to explain. Besides, she probably wouldn't believe me — she and Donner get along perfectly.

"Ready to go?" she asked.

"Sure," I muttered.

Even though she was worried about Granddad, it wasn't hard to see that Marcia couldn't wait to fly that sleigh. Well, she *was* pretty good at it.

"No fancy stuff," I warned.

"Don't worry."

We threw our luggage in the back and climbed into the front seat. I stuck my feet under the foot bars and hung onto the side.

Marcia tried not to smile. Of course, *she* didn't bother. The foot guards are only really necessary when you do fancy maneuvers like loop-the-loops. But unless I needed to hang my head over the side of the sleigh for another reason, I always kept my feet firmly planted under the protection rails.

I defy anyone to call me a coward until they've tried it for themselves.

Marcia slapped the reins, and we moved smoothly off the ground. My stomach lurched more than the sleigh. Even though the sleigh isn't as jerky as a small plane, my lunch quickly threatened to make a reappearance. I tried to make myself believe that my stomach was simply unhappy with the airline food we'd had on the way to Norway.

My stomach didn't believe me.

Half an hour into the flight I had to abandon the safety of the foot rails and let my stomach have its revenge.

As I settled back into the seat, Marcia was staring straight ahead, as though she hadn't noticed. Such nobility is a pain.

"I hope there wasn't anybody beneath us," she said, a deadpan look on her face. Marcia continued. "I think we'd better start carrying airsick bags. Just like the airlines."

"Do whatever you want." I enunciated each word carefully. My stomach was acting up again. "Carry airsick bags. Install a rest room. Hire a stewardess and serve meals. Show an in-flight movie. I don't care."

"What? A movie? With all this beautiful scenery?" She dipped a little to the side so I could see the tundra beneath. I clutched at the side.

"Better yet," I yelped, "install seat belts in this stupid contraption!"

That was it! Seat belts! A strange expression crossed Marcia's face, and we stared at each other.

What if Granddad had fallen out of the sleigh?

CHAPTER 6

Maybe He Fell Out of the Sleigh

"What if he's — " I started to say

"Don't say it!" Marcia yelled.

"Well, he might *not* be. I mean, he usually flies pretty close to the ground."

"Right," she agreed firmly. "Besides, we don't know for sure that's what happened."

No matter what we said, I was scared, and so was Marcia. Granddad wasn't young anymore. If he'd fallen out of the sleigh, he could have broken something. His flight plan crossed deserted country, where there'd be no one to help him. And it was *cold* out there.

Which meant we'd better find him in a big hurry.

* * *

Grandma met us on the field. She was smiling . . . not her usual cheery greeting but more determined. She was trying not to upset us. Despite my queasy stomach, I jumped out and gave her a huge hug.

"Any news?" Marcia demanded.

"No." Grandma's voice quavered only slightly. "I'm glad you're here, kids. Come inside and get warm."

I had to admire her. Grandma wasn't about to break down in front of us. But I could tell how glad she was that we'd arrived.

Not that she'd been alone. The North Pole staff loves my grandparents. Most of them had worked for Santa Claus, Inc. for their whole lives; their parents and grandparents had been employed by the company as well. They were like family. Still, it isn't completely the same.

"We, uh . . . had an idea," I said, once we were settled in front of the huge fireplace with the hot chocolate and cookies Grandma had waiting for us. "We were thinking that maybe . . . or wondering, rather, if it was possible . . . that Granddad might have, uh, fallen out of the sleigh."

Grandma considered it for a few minutes, then nodded slowly.

"It's possible. He made the flight right after

lunch. He usually takes a nap then, but he said he wasn't sleepy. If he dozed off . . ."

We sat staring into the fire.

"Well," I said, "what are we going to do about it?"

"I'm going to take a look at Granddad's flight plan," Marcia declared.

"I'll check out the sleigh," I told her.

On the way out, I picked up a caramel apple. The place was loaded with food. That was Grandma for you — when she got upset or worried, she started cooking.

The apple was for Donner, but don't think I was feeling guilty about what I'd said to him earlier. I wasn't. Besides, he couldn't understand what I'd said. He *is* just a reindeer. My mind told me that, but I couldn't help thinking that Donner knew exactly what was going on.

Anyway, as a peace offering, I brought him the caramel apple. He sniffed it suspiciously, then nearly took my fingers off along with the apple.

I went to inspect the sleigh. Not a thing was out of place. The swing door on the side had a latch, and it seemed to be working perfectly.

"What'd you do?" I heard an anguished cry and looked up to see one of the reindeer wranglers wringing his hands and frantically pulling on Donner's head.

"What's the matter?" I asked, running to the man's side. "Is he sick?" If Donner was sick — mentally ill to my way of thinking — he might have done something to Granddad.

"He's got something in his mouth."

A sick feeling settled in the pit of my stomach. "In his mouth?"

"Yeah. What did you feed him?"

"One of Grandma's caramel apples!" I cried. "He eats them all the time."

The man stuck his gloved hand against Donner's jaw and pulled his mouth open. The apple dropped to the stable floor, the caramel looking rather mashed. Donner's head drooped, and he made that whiny, woofy sound again.

"Poor baby." The man gave me a dark look. "I'm *sure* he didn't mean it."

"Uh . . . uh . . . uh . . . of course not," I gasped. "He loves those things. Granddad gives them to him all the time. Maybe Grandma's recipe was different. I don't know what happened."

The man sniffed, patted Donner, and walked away. Obviously he thought I must have had something to do with the near disaster, something deliberate. I watched him leave, the injustice of it eating at my gut. Why, I'd *never* hurt an animal. At home, my scout troop even collects recyclables to raise money for the local ASPCA.

I felt like a scum-sucking pig.

A crunching noise reached my ears, and I whirled to face Donner. Without a bit of trouble chewing it, he was placidly finishing off the apple.

I felt like calling the reindeer wrangler back but decided it wasn't worth it. Besides, Donner would probably just start choking again.

"It's the last caramel apple you'll ever get from me," I said with great dignity. "Reindeer who lose Santa Claus don't deserve them."

He grunted and glared at me.

"You can't have it both ways," I insisted. "And I may be stupid, but I'm not *that* stupid."

Donner stomped around till his rear end faced me and then . . . well, let's just say he made his point.

CHAPTER 7

The Search Begins

"I'm going to make another pass!" Marcia yelled, the wind whipping her words toward me.

I nodded grimly. It was my job to hang over the side of the sleigh and stare at the ground, searching for any sign of Granddad on the frozen land below. You'd think that being worried about my grandfather and concentrating on finding him would overcome airsickness and being scared of heights. Fat chance.

Admittedly, I was almost numb by now. We'd covered a huge part of Granddad's route without a clue, not a single flash of red. No signals. Nothing. We'd been checking the forested area of northern Canada, the tundra, and the ice cap. I'd seen three zillion trees in the past two days.

Searching was easier in the unforested areas. It hadn't snowed, so we'd be able to see him, unless he'd built an igloo or deviated from his flight plan. He wouldn't do something like that. Or at least we hoped he wouldn't.

"Maybe we should start checking the towns along the way," I said. "What if he's in a hospital somewhere, knocked out?"

"Yeah. Except . . . I hate to go where people are. It's pretty risky."

I gnawed on my knuckles. We'd been searching for two days already. Not only us, but everyone who could be spared was out on foot and snowmobiles. Both our planes were in the air every hour. Yes. We had two planes, but they weren't used much. "Nasty, noisy things," was how Granddad described them.

The sleigh tilted and I gulped. I couldn't shut my eyes, I had to keep watching for Granddad.

"You know," I shouted into the wind, "we can't search these forested areas after dark anyway. What if we went into some towns in the evening?"

"Grandma told us she wants us home for supper," Marcia yelled back at me.

"So? We can eat late."

Marcia didn't answer, but I noticed she started

edging the sleigh south and a little west . . . in the direction of Chicago.

By four in the afternoon it was dark and no use hanging over the side looking for red spots. I sat on the floor of the sleigh to get out of the wind and spread out the map. I pinpointed the towns along Granddad's flight path and showed them to Marcia.

We slid in and out of the first three towns like a charm. Set down. Called the local hospital. Asked a few folks about missing persons, then took off again.

"This is stupid," Marcia said as we headed for our fourth landing. "Mom and Dad have probably already called every town between Chicago and the North Pole."

"Maybe. But we can't be sure unless we check it out for ourselves. Besides, do you have anything better to do?"

In the fourth town, we landed in the city park behind some bushes and trees. As soon as we were grounded, I grabbed my flight bag and groped for some dry crackers to settle my queasy stomach.

Marcia didn't have the heart to rib me about it; she just trudged to the pay phone across the street.

I munched my crackers.

There was some sort of community center across the street; I could see it through the bushes. Suddenly the double doors burst open and a huge group of teenagers ran out, heading in my direction. Standing on the seat, I waved frantically at Marcia. She didn't see me; she was looking in the phone book. And even if she could have seen me, she'd never be able to get back to the sleigh on time.

With a groan, I gingerly picked up the reins. I'd hoped never to touch them again. As firmly as I could, I slapped the leather strips and whispered, "Get going!"

Donner, in the lead, just looked back at me as though he couldn't believe his ears.

"Giddyap!" I hissed, and jerked the reins with what I hoped was an impressive air of authority.

Sluggishly the team rose off the ground, and the sleigh lurched after them. Using what little skills I had, I directed them over some trees — actually, we crunched the top branches — and toward some houses.

One was dark and had a huge backyard and patio. I sure hoped it didn't have one of those motion detector lights. I eased the team into the yard and under the patio cover. No lights. Whew!

"I'll bet you thought I couldn't do it," I said casually, adding for good measure, "Maybe you'll have to treat me with more respect from now on."

I settled back on the seat with a sigh and decided a fifteen-minute wait would give the crowd a chance to clear out. Then I'd head back to the park for Marcia.

When the fifteen minutes were up, I got moving. Leaning forward, I picked up the reins and stared in disbelief. All of them. All *eight* of them!

"Couldn't you find a better place?" I demanded in a whisper. "Did you have to do it on someone's patio?"

It was a fast and firm rule of Santa Claus, Inc., that we never leave anything behind except toys. *Anything.* Including the stuff that comes from the business end of a reindeer. We even carry a scoop and a plastic bag if needed.

"Thanks a lot, guys," I grumbled as I climbed out of the sleigh.

I hesitated as I approached Blitzen. It was only Donner who actually hated me, but the other reindeer weren't exactly fans. To clean up their mess, I had to get awful close to their hind legs. And there wasn't any soft snow on the patio to cushion me.

"Whoa, good fellow," I tried to soothe Blitzen. Scoop. Dump. Scoop. Dump. Eight times. What a disgusting job.

With two fingers I held the bag and snapped it into the compartment. Whew! I climbed into the sleigh and lifted the reins again.

"What took so long?" Marcia asked as she climbed into the sleigh. "It's been clear for almost half an hour."

"Ask your reindeer," I muttered, handing the reins over with pleasure and sitting back in silence. Cleaning up after them was bad enough; I wasn't going to talk about it, too.

CHAPTER 8

More of What I Didn't Know at the Time

"Sorry, mister," the woman at the police desk said. "I checked the computer files, but I didn't find any missing person reports that fit you."

Granddad had felt bad before; now he felt really bad. *No one cared enough to report him missing?*

"Isn't there anything you can do?" he asked.

"Sorry. Without a report, we've got nothing. Check back in, though. Maybe no one's realized you're missing yet. Sometimes it takes a while, you know. Especially if you live alone."

In the meantime, what was he supposed to do?

"Can I call anyone for you?" the woman asked.

"Like who?"

"Oh . . . the Welfare Department, a church — there's some relief organizations."

"I'll . . . let you know."

"Be sure to check back," she told him. "We're still running the fingerprints. It takes time to check with other databases."

He escaped into the outside air with relief, although he had nowhere to go.

"Hi, Santa!" a cheery policeman called as he trotted down the steps.

For a moment he smiled, then it turned into a chuckle, even though it wasn't very funny. Here he was in a town that didn't seem familiar and certainly didn't seem to know *him*. The only thing he owned in the world was a Santa Claus costume. But he wasn't nameless after all. The chuckle rumbled from his chest and burst into an outright laugh.

"Ha-ha-ha-ha!" He held his side and tried to stop. It really *wasn't* funny. Or was it?

"Aren't you supposed to say 'ho, ho, ho'?" a small voice asked. It was a bright-faced boy whose black eyes examined him doubtfully.

Grinning, Granddad obliged. "Ho, ho, ho . . ."

Well, if he took the name of Santa Claus for the time being, at least there was no one who'd object. It wasn't like grabbing the identity of the mayor or someone like that.

And there was no point standing around feeling sorry for himself. He had to do something. He'd been offered a job, two jobs in fact, working as Santa Claus in the mall and over at that department store.

"Pick up your feet, Santa, and get moving!" he told himself.

The mall had offered the highest hourly wage, so he walked there and hunted up the manager, a tired, fussy little man who acted like he wished Christmas would go away.

"Ordinarily, sir," the man explained when Granddad had given him the facts, "ordinarily, we don't hire anyone without some sort of references. And of course, there's the problem of not having a social security number. Hmmmm."

Granddad waited while the manager made a call to the police department. Granddad's fingerprints — while not revealing his identity — had proved him clean of any crimes.

"As I said," the manager continued, finally looking up at Granddad, "we don't normally hire someone just like that. But as I told you yesterday, you do seem perfect for the job. And I'm in quite a fix," the man confessed. "Our usual Santa broke his leg Thanksgiving Day, playing with his grandchildren. Now my father-in-law *and* my uncle *both* want the job and . . . you can see the problem."

"Certainly, certainly."

"You see . . . I could tell them that this unfortunate . . . uh, I mean . . ." The man stuttered to a stop.

"That's all right," Granddad commented smoothly. "Tell them about this poor fellow without a single friend or penny in the world who needed the job desperately. Better not tell them I showed up in a Santa suit. They probably wouldn't believe it."

"Quite right, sir." The man mopped his brow and sighed.

For all his nervous fussiness, the manager turned out to be a pretty decent guy. He gave Granddad a personal loan of fifty dollars and let him use the want ads and a phone to hunt up a place to stay before starting work. By late afternoon, Granddad was back at the mall.

Granddad settled into the Santa throne with a sigh. If he was dressed in a Santa suit, he had to have had experience at this sort of thing, didn't he?

"I wanna baseball bat, and a ball, and a jungle gym, and a car that goes toooot! toooot! toooot!" the kid screamed in his ear.

"Smile!" the woman with the camera said.

Another kid.

"Hey, Santa! I want marbles and a slinky and some bubble gum, and I promise I won't put any gum in Betty's hair anymore, and a teddy bear and a doll and my own bedroom, and I'll keep it clean I promise, and a wagon, and I'll let Betty ride in it, too, and a princess dress and a . . ."

"Smile!" Another picture snapped.

Granddad's knees nearly broke under the next one.

"I want a bike and a thousand tons of candy and a bunk bed and a trip to Disneyland!"

"Smile for Santa!"

"I wanna hundred dolls, more'n Gloria's gonna get, and a ballet dress and a space station and a doctor's kit and a VCR."

"Smile!"

Once a riot broke out because one kid stepped in front of another, and both Granddad and the picture lady had to settle things. He got kicked in the shins. His knees ached. His ears rang from a hundred screaming children.

Were all kids like the ones in this town? Or was Huntsville the only place where a man playing Santa Claus needed accident insurance?

"Santa!" a four-year-old screamed in his ear. "Remember! I want a car that goes toooot! toooot! toooooot!"

Granddad escaped for a break in the employee rest area. "Let me tell you," he announced to the roomful of people, "if I ever get my hands on the guy who invented the idea of Santa Claus, I'll probably wring his neck!"

CHAPTER 9

Caught with Our Sleigh Coming Down

"We can only cover one or two more towns," Marcia said. "It's getting pretty late."

"Okay," I answered. "There's a place called Huntsville. No, wait. Millerton comes before it, and it's even larger."

We found a nice, quiet area behind an elementary school cafeteria to land. Hopefully, a better spot than the last one.

"This time," I announced, "*you* can stay with the team while *I* go and make some calls and look around."

"Sure." Marcia shrugged and lounged back in her seat. "I like it here."

That was the strange thing. She really did like

it. Everything about Santa Claus, Inc., was fun for her. Which seemed weird to me. Then again, Marcia couldn't see why I wanted to mess around with fish and stuff in the ocean, which she thought was icky. According to her, beaches are fine for swimming and picking up shells, but that is all.

I found a telephone booth just down the block in front of a convenience store. I leafed through the book and found the hospital number. No luck. I tried the police station, and the man acted like I was strange, asking if they'd found any missing persons around town lately.

"I'm looking for my grandfather," I explained.

"Sorry, kid," he answered. "No missing persons. Have you filed a missing persons report? I mean, have your parents? Only adults can make a report."

Brother! As if we'd make that mistake again. Except maybe we didn't go about it the right way.

"You see, it's like this. They're out searching, too, and it's just us kids at home right now. We think he might have been flying his plane through this area."

"Oh! Then what you've got to do is check with

his home airport and get his flight plan. They can arrange for a search and rescue."

It wouldn't work. We couldn't make a regular report because there was too much information we couldn't tell them. They'd just get suspicious, like the policewoman in Chicago.

"Thank you, sir," I told the man. "As soon as my parents check back, I'll let them know."

Slowly I replaced the phone and walked into the store. A couple of candy bars would make it look like a casual visit. Besides, Marcia and I had missed supper. Grandma was probably worried sick about us.

"Anything unusual happen around here lately?" I asked.

"Nothin' ever happens in this burg," the clerk told me.

"Well, er . . . my grandfather might have been traveling through here recently, and we haven't seen him. I just wondered if anyone mentioned a stranger."

"Every town's got strangers. Better call the police, kid."

He glanced at his watch and started looking at me rather sharp, so I decided to move along. Maybe the town had a curfew or something for kids.

I sauntered through the door and out of sight before I started running.

"Someone chasing you?" Marcia asked.

"Nope . . . just avoiding curiosity."

She'd just removed a feed bag from Comet's neck.

"Are they finished?" I asked.

"Yep. They were sure hungry."

"Speaking of which." I handed her one of the candy bars I'd bought.

"Thanks. Shall we hit one more town?" she asked.

"Sure. On Donner and Comet, on Cupid and Blitzen, on . . ."

"Oh, shut up."

"On to Huntsville!"

By way of revenge, she made a fast takeoff, and my stomach lurched. I was glad I hadn't eaten that candy bar yet.

Huntsville was probably a quiet town most of the time, but not during the Christmas season. Every store in the place was lit up like . . . well, a Christmas tree. The downtown was still swarming with people. I glanced at my watch and was surprised to find it was only 8:45.

"Look for another school," I advised.

We edged over a group of houses in a slow glide, looking for a likely place. Marcia spotted another school and dropped toward it.

One foot off the ground, we heard a voice.

"Wow! Look at that!"

We landed with a lurch and were suddenly surrounded. Obviously, we'd misjudged the security of our landing site.

"That's incredible."

"Those look like real reindeer!"

"But where's Santa Claus?"

"It's amazing!"

There was a sick look on Marcia's face. I'd hate to have seen my own at the moment. The only unbreakable rule of security was *Don't get caught!*

We were caught.

"Is that really Santa's sleigh?" a kid demanded.

"It's unbelievable!" a woman's voice marveled.

"And to think I never believed in Santa," a man commented.

"Where's Santa Claus?" the kid demanded again.

"It's not like that, really," Marcia faltered. Her face had turned a sickly white.

"Why didn't I bring my video camera?" a man moaned. "This'd hit the six o'clock news like gang-busters."

The news. Media. Lights. Camera. *Action!* That was it!

"Glad we made such a splash!" I said with enthusiasm. "The special effects boys'll be thrilled."

"Special effects?" one woman asked.

"You bet! It's a new company, and we're hoping to rival some of the big guys on *this* picture."

"You're making a movie?" the boy asked, disappointment in his face.

"We sure are."

"Aren't you kind of young for this kind of job?" an older man demanded.

"Well, my dad says it's a young person's game. Besides, we're just filling in until the rest of the team gets back from the restaurant."

"That's pretty cool, though," said a girl about my age.

"Yeah. I'm glad to get in on the ground floor. There's a lot of money in this business."

"Might have known it'd turn out to be a movie," a woman commented. "That's probably what that other guy . . ."

"But where're the movie cameras?" a teenager demanded.

"Oh," I answered breezily, "they're finished with this scene, so they put the cameras away. When they get back, we'll load up and get on the road again."

"Shoot! I thought I might get a job as an extra."

"Do you folks have a permit for this kind of thing?" a stuffy-looking gentleman interrupted.

"I wouldn't know, sir," I answered with a dead-pan expression. "I'm just a kid."

"Well, they'd *better* have one."

"They . . . they do," Marcia finally spoke up. "I heard them talking about it at lunch."

"Say," a young man exclaimed, "how'd you pull it off, the sleigh flying and such?"

"Sorry, mister." I threw a look of regret onto my face. "We can't let out trade secrets."

"Sure, I understand. But it was pretty convincing."

"I'll tell our special effects manager. He'll be pleased; after all, they put enough money into the project."

One by one the crowd walked away.

"I still wish I'd brought my camera," a voice drifted back.

"I can't wait to see that movie. . . . Hey, kid!" a man called, "what's the movie going to be called?"

"Uh . . ." I hesitated. "It can still change, but I think it's called *Santa S.O.S.*"

Finally, everyone was gone.

For once I didn't mind a quick exit into the air.

CHAPTER 10

I Had a Feeling I Was Missing Something

We made it back to the North Pole in record time. I wasn't worth much by the time we arrived. Grandma was waiting for us in the stable.

"Where have you two been?" she demanded. She wasn't all weak and trembly like I'd expected.

"We . . . er . . . decided to check out some towns on the flight path," I explained.

"Humph!" she muttered, and walked out of the stable. I could have sworn she was smiling, except I couldn't see her face. Trust Grandma; she'd probably figured out what we were doing the whole time.

"She's not mad," Marcia said with wide eyes.

"Nope. But we might have to rustle up our own supper."

Fortunately, we didn't have to unharness the reindeer or bed them down for the night. The staff would handle it. Even so, Marcia went forward and started making mushy sounds to the team. She was yawning like crazy — Marcia isn't a night person like me. Still, I figured she'd be at it for a while, so I set my teeth and rushed for the house; it is *cold* at the North Pole at ten P.M. in December.

I was wrong about supper. Grandma handed me a plate as soon as I walked into the kitchen. It didn't look warmed over, either.

"Looks like you expected us to get back late," I told her.

"You're not my grandson for nothing."

"It was my fault, you know. I'm the one who talked Marcia into it."

"I figured as much. Although you probably didn't have to twist her arm."

I mused on this while I ate. Having everything turned upside down, I was seeing things in a different way than usual. Take Grandma, for example. There she was, bustling around like it was in the middle of the day. Of course, in the wintertime up at the North Pole, it is always pretty dark, so day and night kind of get confused. But it had never seemed to affect bedtime before, for me at least.

Marcia dragged herself in and slumped at the table. She seemed barely awake enough to chew and swallow. After a few bites, she excused herself and drifted out the door. I was on my second plate.

Grandma was starting a batch of cookies. *Starting*. Not finishing.

"I always thought you were a morning person, like Granddad and Dad and Mom," I commented.

"Like I said, Nicky, you're not my grandson for nothing."

You know, I hadn't appreciated Grandma enough till lately. She'd surprised us all, the way she stood up for Marcia and me, so Marcia could be Santa Claus and I could be an oceanographer. I'd always felt like the odd one out in my family. But maybe I wasn't the only one after all.

"Say, Grandma," I asked. "If you hadn't married Granddad, what would you have done?"

"Women didn't really have careers in those days, Nicky. We all just expected to get married and raise families."

"Okay. What if you'd been born later?"

"I'd still have married your grandfather. And . . ."

"Yeah?"

"I rather think I might have been an oceanographer on the side."

Even with our late night, Marcia and I were up early. It was the only time in my life that getting up by seven in the morning wasn't torture. I woke up and started thinking about Granddad, and then I couldn't go back to sleep.

"Hi, kids," Grandma greeted us when we came into the kitchen. "How about a good, hearty breakfast to start the day?"

I glanced out the window. It was dark, and it felt like the times Dad got us up at three A.M. to drive to the mountains for a fishing trip or something.

Grandma's face was calm, but there were dark circles under her eyes. Maybe she hadn't even gone to bed at all; there were three cakes on the sideboard I couldn't remember seeing last night.

"Sounds good, Grams," I told her.

Grandma's idea of a hearty breakfast this morning included oatmeal, scrambled eggs, ham, hash browns, pancakes, orange juice, and milk. If we were still hungry, she said, after pushing second helpings on us, there were some cinnamon rolls nearly ready to put into the oven.

"Sounds great," Marcia said. "Can we take some in the sleigh? For a snack."

"I've got a big sack lunch all ready for you," Grandma answered. "But I'll wrap the cinnamon rolls and put them on top before you leave."

"Big enough for two meals?" I asked her with a sudden grin.

"Maybe," she said. "Maybe."

Marcia left to do her preflight check. That was her responsibility, not mine.

Besides, something was bothering me. I had this nagging sensation that I'd missed something.

I really hate that feeling.

That was what woke me up so early. This dream came, and it was like I could see a woman mouthing some words, but I couldn't make out what she was saying. Then someone else said, "You dummy! Good thing *you're* not going to be Santa Claus." Everyone started laughing, and I glanced down and realized I was only wearing pajamas with teddy bears on them. "Say it again," I shouted to the woman, "say it louder." Her lips moved again, but I couldn't hear a thing.

"Your sister tells me you two had quite an adventure last night," Grandma said as she took the cinnamon rolls from the oven and wrapped them with foil first, then with a towel to keep them warm.

"Which one?" I asked.

"What I heard," she said, "was that you did

some quick thinking and got the two of you out of a sticky mess."

When she wasn't being obnoxious, Marcia could be a pretty nice sister.

"Oh, that one," I answered with a modest air. "That was nothing . . . nothing any genius couldn't handle."

"I'm impressed. Even if you are a good-for-nothing smart aleck. You're my grandson, so you might be a genius after all. Of course, your flying takes you down a peg or two."

"I think I'll be all right, especially since the average person isn't judged by how well he or she can fly Santa's sleigh."

"Lucky for you."

CHAPTER 11

Where I Figure Out What I Was Missing

It was getting harder and harder to keep my hopes up. Not only me. Everyone.

The North Pole staff wandered around in a feverish daze, frantically rushing when there was something to do and staring into space the rest of the time.

We'd limited search crews to six-hour shifts, but they kept stretching their time limits, then wanted to go back out after only five or six hours of sleep.

In spite of everything, it was rather nice, seeing how everyone was working together and helping one another.

Get a grip! I told myself. *Pretty soon you'll be as*

mushy as Marcia, and then where'll you be? You gotta be tough, for Grandma.

I couldn't wait to get to the barn and see Donner. I could count on him to take the sentiment out of anything. And toss it to the floor and step on it.

One whiff of the enclosed space with all those reindeer and my eyes started watering and my nose started itching.

"All set?" I asked, and deliberately sauntered past Donner. Marcia wasn't looking; he aimed a swift hind leg at my shins. But for once I was too quick! Score one for Nick.

"Does Grandma think we're football players?" Marcia asked as I loaded the lunch supplies into an empty toy compartment.

"She just doesn't want us to wait till ten o'clock in the evening to eat, like last night," I said.

"Grams gave us permission to search more towns?"

"What do you call *six* extra sandwiches? An order to be home at five?"

Marcia's forehead creased. "I don't want to have any close calls like last night."

"What're you talking about?"

"We're just lucky they believed you and thought it was a big movie stunt."

I almost had it then . . . a niggling, nagging feeling. Doggone it! Why couldn't I grab hold of it and figure out what was bothering me?

"Hey, Marcia. Do you have the feeling we've missed something, some clue to where Granddad is?"

Her brown eyes opened, and her eyebrows arched in surprise. "What do you mean? We've done everything possible. Short of calling in the army."

"I know. It's just that I have a feeling I'm missing something, and if I could only figure it out, we'd be able to find him."

"Wish you could."

Marcia climbed into the sleigh, and I followed, dumping myself on the seat like a sack of potatoes.

When lunchtime came, Marcia grounded. For herself, she could have driven with one hand and eaten a sandwich with the other. But she decided the reindeer needed a rest. Of course, the reindeer don't do all of the work pulling the sleigh forward, they just work with the antigrav stuff that our ancestor invented. But even if they don't actually do the flying, being in the air too long is hard on their equilibrium.

Marcia ate a big lunch. I nibbled a few soda crackers.

"With these short days," I said, "it's going to be

dark in a couple of hours. Maybe we should hit Huntsville first."

"Are you crazy?" Marcia demanded. "We'd have to be nuts to go back there. What if we're seen again and someone starts wondering whether there's something more going on than special effects?"

"If we're really going to cover the towns on Granddad's flight path," I answered, "we have to go to Huntsville next. We didn't get a chance to check anything or ask any questions."

"They asked *us* plenty of questions!"

I dropped it for the moment. Admittedly, it was a risk going back to Huntsville. But heading into any town was a risk. At least those folks already had an explanation for it.

There it was again! Nibbling on the edge of my brain. A woman. A woman saying something. "Might have known it'd turn out to be a movie. That's probably what that other guy . . ."

That other guy.

"What other guy?" I asked aloud.

"What d'ya mean, what other guy?"

"The woman last night. She started saying something about what that other guy was doing. The way she talked, it *had* to be something connected with Santa Claus. That's it, Marcia. We have to go back there."

"Okay, if you insist." I guess she was too discouraged to argue. She brushed the crumbs away and started to repack the lunch. "Are you sure you don't want a roast beef sandwich?" she asked, and waved one in front of my nose.

"You have a sadistic streak," I answered with dignity, and gulped down my heaving stomach.

CHAPTER 12

Where I Began Finding Out What I Didn't Know Before

"I wanna stuffed giraffe big enough so's I can sit on it, and a water pistol, and a great big hat like a cowboy!"

Santa wondered how many kids had rotated on and off his lap in the last three days. His knees were beginning to buckle under the strain. And his ears were giving out as well. Why did so many of the children think they had to yell into his ear? Yell? More like *scream*.

"Gimme a bike and some roller skates and a horse and my own room!"

The manager of the mall had made it clear that Santa was *not* to ask about whether the children were naughty or nice. After all, the stores wanted to sell toys and didn't care whether the kids who got them were little monsters.

"Hey, Santa!!!!" a four-year-old boy yelled in his ear. "Didn't ya hear me? I wanna train and a truck and a new brother instead of that baby sister."

"Sorry, young fellow," he chuckled, and ho-ho-hoed a little. "The sister's here to stay, but we'll see what we can do about the rest."

The mother gave him a grateful look before hauling herself, the crying baby, and her son off into the crowd.

Brother! Was he ever grateful when they told the children Santa had to have a ten-minute break.

When he emerged from the employee lounge, a boy and girl were waiting just outside. Their faces brightened, and they jumped forward. Great. Just great. These kids were old enough to know better.

"Granddad!" the boy exclaimed, and the girl cast herself into his arms.

"We were so worried!"

Were these his grandchildren? Strange. Did they look at all familiar? Maybe a little. Of course, he'd seen about a million children in the past few days.

"Hi, kids," he said, setting the girl upright again.

"We'd better get going," she told him. "We left the sleigh in an empty shed. It's pretty deserted, but we shouldn't take any chances."

"Sleigh?" he questioned.

The faces of the two children reddened. "Yeah," the boy explained uneasily. "We've been using the sleigh to search the towns all the way from Chicago. But we've been *real* careful!"

"We can get you back to the North Pole in no time," the girl added cheerily.

"Nice try, kids," he told them. "But I've got to get back to work."

"Nice try?" the girl asked.

"What're you talking about, Granddad?" the boy questioned.

"Look. You two are old enough to stop playing games about Santa Claus. And I've really got to get back. I'm only on a break."

"But . . ."

Without waiting for more, he hurried across to the Santa throne. It was disappointing. For a moment, he thought he'd been found.

"Santa!!!!!!" a dozen kids yelled.

Oh! For some peace and quiet!

With mouths open, Marcia and I stared at Granddad's back as he walked away from us. This was terrible!

My hunch had proved correct. We'd landed in Huntsville, and I'd left Marcia with the team while I checked out the police. Sure enough, they'd had a missing person in a Santa Claus suit! With amnesia. It had to be Granddad, and the amnesia explained why he hadn't called anyone.

No problem, I had thought. *We'll go down to the mall, and when Granddad sees us he'll remember who he is. Everything'll be fine. We might even get back to the North Pole in time for a late supper!*

I decided it would be better to phone Mom and Dad after we found him. There was no way to call Grandma direct from a pay phone.

I never dreamed Granddad wouldn't recognize us!

"Hey!" Marcia nudged me. "We'd better call Mom and Dad to tell them Granddad's all right."

"*That's* all right?"

She paused and studied the scene. The place was mobbed with kids. Little ones crawling on the floor, some with runny noses. Three four-year-olds were trying to climb onto the plastic reindeer, and one kid with a *really* smelly diaper sat on the floor about three feet away from me. Another kid about six looked like he was going to burp up his ice cream cone.

In the middle of all this Granddad sat on Santa's throne while a line of children waited to sit on his lap and tell him everything they wanted for Christmas. It did *not* look like Grand-dad was enjoying himself. In fact, he looked downright miserable.

"I can't believe he didn't know us," Marcia said. "And he acted like we were trying to play a trick."

"Yeah," I agreed. "After all, he doesn't know that he isn't just playing Santa Claus, he really *is* Santa. In fact . . ." I paused and considered what he'd said to us. "I have a feeling he doesn't be-lieve in Santa Claus."

Marcia looked at me and started to giggle.

CHAPTER 13

When I Get to Sit on Santa's Lap

"Amnesia!" Dad exclaimed over the phone. "This isn't a joke, is it Nick? You mean he really doesn't remember who he is?"

"Not only that," I couldn't resist telling my father, "he doesn't believe in Santa Claus anymore."

"He . . . what?"

"He doesn't believe in Santa Claus. And something else . . ." I paused dramatically. "I don't think he enjoys being Santa. At least it doesn't look like it."

"Don't be silly," Dad pooh-poohed the idea.

"Just ask Marcia." I handed the receiver to my sister. She admitted, reluctantly, that Granddad without his memory was a normal person who didn't believe in Santa Claus and didn't enjoy kids screaming in his ears.

Okay. So sue me. Now that I knew Granddad was safe, I was getting a little fun out of the situation. A few months ago, when I said I didn't want to be Santa Claus someday, most of the family had acted like I was crazy — and a traitor — and an ungrateful brat.

"It's the greatest job in the world!" Granddad was in the habit of saying. "Santa adds to the joy of Christmas. He's become a symbol of generosity and kindness."

"Christmas would survive," I had protested, "even without Santa Claus."

He'd looked at me sideways and stomped off. He didn't like being reminded that his job was not indispensable.

Granddad finally accepted the idea of Marcia being Santa, mostly because Grandma thought it was the right thing. Besides, Marcia is really good at the Santa Claus gig. And she doesn't get airsick. But Granddad still acted like I was an ungrateful brat who wouldn't know a good thing if it jumped up and bit me. Which isn't true. I know it's a good job — for Marcia. And oceanography's a good job — for me.

Marcia finally hung up the phone.

"So what's our plan of action?" I inquired. "Do

we kidnap him and introduce Santa to his reindeer?"

"Impractical," she answered. "We'd never get him away from all those children."

"In that case, let's try to jog his memory some more." I sauntered back to the Santa Claus area and got into the line. Some of the mothers looked at me with frowns. I could guess what they were thinking — either I was too old to still believe in Santa, or maybe they wondered if I was going to rip off his beard and spoil the illusions of their children. Marcia seemed embarrassed; I was enjoying myself.

After an hour we reached the head of the line. Granddad's eyes narrowed as he looked at me, but he couldn't say anything, not with a bunch of rug rats listening in.

"Hi, Santa!" I said with a grin, and sat lightly on his lap. He grunted even so. "You know what I'd like for Christmas?" I asked.

"No, what?" he grunted again, shifting underneath me. After all, I was considerably heavier than the average six-year-old.

"How about some books on the ocean? That's what I really want. More than anything else in the world, I want to be an oceanographer. I want to study the ocean and get rid of pollution and fix the ozone layer. My family had other ideas for me," I confessed. "They wanted me to go into the family business, which I consider a pain in the neck, but they're going to let my sister take up the reins instead."

He regarded me with a sour look but still without any recognition.

"And I'd love something about computers for Christmas," I continued. "You love computers, *don't* you, Santa? I'll bet you're up on the latest technology. Say, you must have put the entire world into a program, so you'd know what people asked for next year and whether they're naughty or nice."

Marcia choked and I avoided her eyes. Computers were a sore spot for Granddad, if he'd only remember.

"Don't you, Santa?" I asked again. "Don't you just *love* computers?"

"Er . . ." He didn't seem to know what to say, so I tried another subject.

"By the way," I asked, "what is it you use to get the sleigh to fly? Is it some kind of antigrav, or is it just plain magic?"

Marcia gave me a warning frown, but I ignored her. There wasn't any danger. They all thought that I was just a pushy kid with an overactive imagination.

"And what would happen," I inquired, "if you

or someone in your family was allergic to reindeer?"

At that point he must have signaled someone. A girl dressed like a green elf came over and suggested I might like a candy cane and that it was time to let someone else have a turn with Santa Claus.

"Nice try," Marcia said as we walked away.

"We'll give it another shot tomorrow."

"We can't leave him here!"

"We can't spend the night, either, and the mall is closing in half an hour. Come on, Marcia! He's been okay here all week. We should go back to the North Pole and get some pictures or something to jog his memory. Or maybe Grandma should come back with us."

"*Another* trip into town with the sleigh? Granddad's going to kill us."

"He's got to remember us first."

CHAPTER 14

Someone's Got to Do It

Grandma stood with her arms crossed over her stomach and stared at Granddad. She'd had her arms crossed that way ever since we left the North Pole.

We'd managed to stop Granddad as he came out of the employee rest area.

"You again!" he'd growled.

"Nicholas," Grandma said.

He'd looked at her with a frown, then shrugged and walked away.

"You looked familiar to him," Marcia said. "I could tell."

"Of course. That's why he was so overjoyed to see me!" Grandma snapped.

I didn't bother trying to play games around

Grandma. You might pull it off with Granddad, and for *sure* my parents, but I'd learned that you couldn't get around Grandma that way.

"Come on." I followed Granddad back to the Santa area. Even if he didn't remember us, we were going to be a familiar sight from now on.

We'd been watching him for about an hour when I glanced at Grandma and saw her lips twitching. She nudged Marcia. "Well, well. You or your dad may inherit the job sooner than you expected. When your grandfather gets his memory back, he just might be ready to retire."

Marcia's eyes twinkled. Underneath, of course, we were all still worried. It'd be horrible if Granddad never remembered who he was.

"I have an idea," I suggested. "Let's start a riot and sneak him out of here in all the confusion."

So help me, at that exact moment, a riot *did* start. On my honor, I had nothing to do with it.

"Last year you *promised*!" a kid's voice yelled. "I wanted a train and you brought me a truck!"

A kid stood on the wide railing around the throne. His face was red, and he was stomping his foot. It was probably his mother who was grabbing for him, but he jumped away from her and snatched a handful of candy canes from the elf lady. He started pelting the canes at Granddad.

In less than ten seconds, all the kids in the place were screaming their heads off. Most were trying to protect Granddad, I think. But when they rushed the platform, they knocked over the sleigh and the cardboard reindeer.

The kid on the railing jumped down, but I still saw candy canes flying at Granddad's head.

"Stop! Stop!! Stop!!! STOP!!!!" Granddad's voice rose above the roaring crowd. "BE QUIET!!!!!" he yelled.

Slowly, the kids backed off and mothers grabbed them and the kids fell silent. It wasn't so much that Granddad had told them to be quiet. No, I think it was because his face was turning red, then purple. He looked ready to explode, and every eye in the place was glued on him.

In the eerie silence, one last candy cane flew through the air and rebounded off his forehead.

"Naughty," he stated clearly and carefully, before stomping back to his throne. He gripped the arms and lifted the chair an inch or so before thunking himself into the seat.

It was the last straw for the display. The Santa's Castle gave a sigh and fell forward.

It hit Granddad dead center.

I rushed in, trying to get to Granddad and trying not to squash any kids in the process. Fighting my way to the platform, I started heaving broken pieces of Santa's Castle off my grandfather. Fortunately, they weren't too heavy, but I was scared what they might have done to Granddad's head.

Finally I got to him. There wasn't any blood. Only a red dent on his forehead.

"Granddad!" I yelled.

His eyes opened.

"Nick," he groaned.

My legs turned to rubber, and I sat down fast.

"Yeah, Santa?" I asked.

"Be an oceanographer," he said. "It's safer."

Under the circumstances, the mall manager didn't insist that Granddad stay on the job. They had to close down for a couple of days anyway, to make repairs.

"It's just as well you got your memory back," the manager told Granddad. "I don't think you're cut out to be Santa Claus."

With that, we marched out of the mall and hurried back to the sleigh. Marcia and Granddad sat in the front seat while Grandma and I sat in the back, both of us with our arms folded hard against our middles. As we took off, I remembered there were still eighteen shopping days till Christmas. Plenty of time to cash in on flower delivery tips.

*   *   *

For the rest of the season I was at my most charming. Between my smiles, freckles, and the Christmas spirit, I made a tidy income. I even beat Marcia in our bet.

"I'd have won if we weren't interrupted," Marcia said when she paid me the ten dollars.

"I was interrupted, too," I answered.

"Humphhh!"

And I'm glad to say that Granddad did learn a few things from his experience. For one thing, he had more of a sense of humor about Santa Claus, Inc. "It's a dangerous job," he said with a sideways grin at me, "but someone's got to do it."

"How'd you come to fall out of the sleigh?" Grandma asked.

"Er . . ." he hesitated (talk about your rosy cheeks!). "I don't really know. I sort of . . . dozed off."

I tried not to laugh. I really did.

But my greatest triumph was what he said next.

"One thing is sure," he announced. "As soon as possible, I'm having seat belts installed in that sleigh!"